I0751684

Published by Zara Press
First published 2026
ISBN: 978-2-87996-279-5

What Remains of Her Voice

Margaux Zara

Book I 7
I. Before 8
II. The Punishment 22
III. Narcissus 33
IV. The Dissolution 49
V. What Remains 58
Interlude: The Crossing 67
Book II 71
I. Kore 72
II. The Taking 91
III. The Underworld 99
V. The Return 145
VI. Queen 162
Author's Note 171

No one, either of the deathless gods
or of mortal men,
heard her voice.

— Homeric Hymn to Demeter

Book I

Echo

I. Before

i.

They say a woman
should take up less space than her shadow.

I filled rooms before I entered them.

My voice was the thing that arrived first —
preceding me like the smell of something burning,
lingering in the room,
before I did.

Men called it too much.
I called it mine.

I knew how to make silence
last longer than it wanted to.
How to pull a story
by its tail
until it gave.

Even the gods forgot themselves
long enough to listen.

What they don't tell you
is that I knew what I was doing.

Zeus with his restless hands,
Hera with her watching eyes —
I stood between them
and I talked.

Not out of innocence.
Out of something older than that.
Something that knew the shape of a favour
before it was asked.

Maybe there is no better name for it.

I called it survival.
I called it pleasure.
Some days I could not tell the difference.

ii.

There is a pleasure in it
you would not understand
unless you have felt a word
move through you
before it leaves

the way hollow sits low in the throat,
the way silver arrives already bright,
the way hunger means exactly
what it feels like to say.

I spoke the way water moves.
Not thinking direction.
Just following the shape
of whatever held me.

Sometimes I would find a word
and turn it over like a stone
to see what lived beneath

all that darkness,
all that wet.

The nymphs grew tired of my mouth.
The trees did not.

I have spent whole afternoons
giving names back to things
that had forgotten them

the specific grey of light
before it decides to be morning,
the weight a body holds
when grief has just arrived
and not yet made itself at home.

I was good at this.

I want you to know that
before you hear what came next —

I was good at this.

iii.

Here is what I will not pretend:

I knew where he went
when I kept her at the gate of words.

Hera, her eyes like the flat of a blade,
her patience a country
I had learned to move through
carefully,
on foot.

I would begin a story
and she would follow
that was her flaw,
if gods can be said to have them.

She could not resist
an unfinished thing.

Neither could I.

I told myself it was just language —
the mouth doing what it does,
filling space,
making time.

But I watched her face
and I knew the shape of a door
before I reached it.

What do you do
with knowledge you still choose.

You learn to hold it differently.
You learn to rename it.

I never asked what happened in the hills.

Some things stay cleaner
in the not-asking.

iv.

The afternoon I remember most
I was doing nothing.

Sitting at the edge of the creek
where water argues with itself
over stones.

I was thinking about a word
susurrus
how it sounds like what it is,
how rare that is,
for a thing to carry
its own description.

A bird landed close.
I didn't move.
It looked at me
the way small creatures do
deciding.

Then left.

The light was doing
what late light does
making everything
briefly
precious.

I let it.

I did not know
this was the last time
my thoughts would arrive
in my own words.

I did not know
because it was
an ordinary afternoon

and ordinary afternoons
do not announce themselves.

They end.

v.

They loved me the way you love
a fire in a room

grateful for the warmth,
careful of the edge.

I made them laugh.
I made them lean in.
I made the long afternoons
pass like something
other than waiting.

But I saw it —
the laugh held a beat too long,
admiration with a shadow
it would not name.

Callisto braided my hair once
and said:
you make everything
so easy.

She meant it kindly.

I heard what lived beneath it
the faint exhaustion
of standing next to someone
who takes up exactly
as much space as she wants.

I did not make myself smaller.

I considered it once
for less than a breath.

Then I opened my mouth
and the afternoon
filled up again.

vi.

I understood early
that every room has a current —

the way water moves
beneath water,
invisible unless you know
what to look for.

Olympus was no different,
only larger,
only heavier with force.

Power did not move in thunderbolts.
It moved in proximity.
In small negotiations.

Who stood near whom.
Who spoke first.
Who watched the door.

Zeus was easy to read —
desire always is.
It moves in straight lines.

Hera was harder.
She had learned stillness
while everything inside her
moved.

I respected that.

I knew what standing between them required —
a balance that looks like grace
from far away
and feels like pressure up close.

I made it look like grace.

vii.

I watched her when she didn't know.

Which was never.
She always knew.

That was Hera —
she received everything
and returned nothing.

A closed system.
A fist that had forgotten
how to open.

Once, at the edge of a gathering,
I saw her laugh —
not the performance,
the thing itself
arriving before she could shape it.

For a moment she was only
a woman
finding something funny.

Then Zeus crossed the room
and her face closed.

I kept it.
Filed it away in the dark.

I did not know it would be her hand
that reached for me later.

II. The Punishment

i. Hera

Do not speak to me of jealousy
as though it is a small thing.

As though I sit on my throne
picking at a wound
out of vanity.

I have watched him
for centuries.

The particular way he leaves
not sneaking,
never sneaking,
walking as though the world
was made to accommodate him.

It was.
That is the problem.

You want me to be above it.
A goddess should be above it.

I am above it
the way a mountain
is above the weather
that still tears it apart.

I have swallowed so much
that I have forgotten
what an empty mouth feels like.

She is not the first.
She will not be the last.

But she stood at my gate
with her bright tongue
and her knowing eyes
and she chose.

Not innocently.
She chose.

So yes.

I reached into her
and took the thing
she loved most about herself.

Tell me you wouldn't.

ii.

It wasn't loud.

I expected loud.
A goddess's rage should arrive
decisive,
like the sky deciding.

It was more like
a hand closing
around a flame.

One moment
the word already forming,
warm in the throat,
already mine

and then
the shape of it,
without the word inside.

I opened my mouth.

What came back
was not mine.

I stood very still
the way you stand
when you are not yet sure
what has been taken.

Testing the edges of it
with my tongue
like a socket
where a tooth was.

The creek still argued with itself over stones.
The bird did not return.
The light was doing
what late light does.

iii.

I tried, at first,
the way you try a door
you already know is locked —
not from hope
but from the need to be certain.

A word arrived.
I reached for it.

It passed through me
and kept going
and came back
wearing someone else's mouth.

This is the thing about loss
it has to be tested
over and over
before the body believes it.

I said: here.
Someone else had said here first
and the sound came back
just that
just the address of a place
nobody home.

I said: I am
The hill returned it —
I am, I am —

but it did not know
what it was saying.
I said:

Narcissus

The hill said:

cissus

us

I said: look at me —
look —
me

I had thought my voice was something I had.

I understood then
it was something I was.

iv.

The first morning was the worst

not because of grief
grief I could have held
grief has a shape
a weight you can learn
to distribute

It was the small things

A nymph asking
which way the river path ran
and my mouth
opening around the answer

the river path —

just the end of her question
handed back
useless
a door that only opens
from one side

The look on her face
confusion first.
then something quieter
the adjustment.

the moment a person
reclassifies you

I had been
the one who filled rooms

I became
the one people
spoke carefully around
the way you speak
around something fragile
something that might
embarrass you
if it breaks
in front of everyone

But I had always been
most myself
in language.

Without it
I was a house
with all the lights off

still standing.
nobody home.

They didn't mean to be cruel.

That is what I want to say first.

Cruelty with intention can be met.
This was softer.
Avoidance dressed as care.

the conversations
that stopped
just before I arrived,
the careful way
they chose their words
around me,
simplified,
slowed down,
as though I had lost
not just my voice
but my understanding.

Phoebe stopped mid-story once
when she saw me coming.

"Never mind", she said,
"It's not important."

It was important.
I saw it still alive in her face.

She chose not to give it to me.

That is what nobody tells you
About losing your voice:

But she had already
turned the conversation
somewhere easier.

That is what nobody tells you
about losing your voice —

it is not only
that you cannot speak.

It is that people stop speaking to you.

I watched them from outside
Of every conversation I used to hold.

I had become
the absence inside language
before I became its echo.

III. Narcissus

I.

I heard him before I saw him.

His voice carrying through the trees
the way certain sounds do —
not loud,
just inevitable,
the way thunder arrives
already inside your chest.

I should say something dignified here.
That I observed him.
That I considered.

He stepped into the light
and my new mouth
opened around nothing.

All that careful silence
and still —
the body,
doing what the body does,
wanting without permission.

He was beautiful
the way unfinished things are —
as though the world
had not yet decided
what to do with him.

I did not know then
that he was the same.
That he too
stood at the edge of himself
unable to enter.

That we were the same wound
expressed differently —

me, all voice and no mirror.
him, all mirror and no voice.

ii.

He said: is anyone there?

And I, who was entirely there,
who was only there,
gave him back:
anyone there

He said: come to me.

And I crossed the distance
between one heartbeat and the next,
stepped into the open
with everything I had —

and gave him:
come to me —

the words arriving between us
like an offering
he thought he'd made himself.

He looked past me.

Not through me
past.
The specific geometry of a gaze
that has already decided
what is worth landing on.

He said: I would rather die
than give myself to you.

And I, with nothing left
but his own words
to answer him,

gave him back the only part
I could bear to return —

to you —

carried it home in my mouth
like something broken,

held it there
long after he had gone.

To you
To you
To you

The water is the only thing
that has ever looked at me
the way I needed to be looked at.

Not because I am vain —
I want to correct that story.

Because every other face
has always wanted something back.

She was there again today.
I could feel her
the way you feel weather
a pressure,
a waiting.

I don't know what she wants me to do
with that.

The water wants nothing.
The water just —
receives me.

I have been so tired
for so long
of being looked at
by things that need.

The water never needs.

I know this is not
a solution.

I know somewhere
in the part of me
that is still capable
of knowing things

this is not
a solution.

But I am so tired.

And the water
is right there.

And it is the only place
in the world
where I can look
and not be asked
for anything
in return.

iii.

It came on a Tuesday.

Or what would have been a Tuesday —
the kind of day
that has no intention of being significant,
grey and unremarkable,
a day the world made
just to fill the space
between better days.

He passed me on the path.

I had been waiting —
not dramatically,
just the way a tree waits for lightning —
whole body already adjusted to the blow.

He passed me
and his eyes moved across me
the way eyes move across
a tree,
a stone,
an arrangement of air —

acknowledging only
that something occupied the space,
not what.

And I understood
with the particular clarity
of a thing
you have known for a long time
finally arriving in your chest —

that I was not
a person to him.

Not even a body.

Just the world
doing what the world does —
existing
in his periphery.

I did not collapse.
I did not rage.

I simply stood on the path
after he had gone
and let the knowing
settle into me
like sediment.

iv.

Let me be precise about it.

Not the large version —
not the sweep of it
the mythology of longing
people reach for
when they want to sound
like they have suffered beautifully.

The small version.

The way I arranged myself
on the riverbank
at the angle
I had calculated
was most likely
to catch his eye.

The way I practised, in my head,
the words I would have said —
the perfect ones,
the ones that would have made him
turn and really look —

and then the silence
where they should have been.

The way I memorised
the specific way he moved through trees —
unhurried
as though the world
had agreed in advance
to accommodate his pace.

The way hope works —
not as a single flame
but as something that keeps
relighting itself
in the dark,

stubborn and stupid
and essential

the way the body keeps breathing
without being asked.

I am not ashamed of the wanting.

It was real —
it had specific gravity
specific texture
it lived in my chest
like a stone
that had learned
to be warm.

v.

Ianthe saw

She watched me follow him
through the birch trees
one afternoon —

I did not know she was there
which means
my face was doing
what faces do
when they forget
to perform composure

She told me later
— later, when later was all I had —
that it had been
both painful
and clarifying
to watch

You looked like someone, she said,
trying to pour water
into a closed hand.

I wanted to be angry at her
the clean release of it —
someone to direct it toward,
a face to give the feeling

But she was right
She had seen it plainly
from the outside
the way you cannot see
what you are standing inside of

We have a name for what she saw —
but names don't help much
when you are standing in the birch trees
with your whole heart
aimed at someone
already elsewhere.

She held my hand that evening
said nothing.

vi.

It took longer
than you would think.

He came back to the pool
the way people return
to the thing that is killing them —
with relief
with the peace of stopping resistance.

I stayed at a distance.

I watched him speak to it.

The face in the water
gave him back everything he offered —
every word, every gesture, every longing.

I understood then
something I had missed:

we were not so different —
the pool and I.

Both of us
returning only what was given.
Both of us
unable to originate.

The difference was this:

the pool did not love him.

It was only water
reflection without intent.

I did.

I was the one
who stood on the bank
with something real to give
and no way to give it

watching him choose
his own face
over and over

until there was
nothing left of him
to choose.

When it was over
I did not move
for a long time.

The pool held his absence
without preference

I stood there
and I grieved for both of us.

For him — that he never got out
of himself.

For me — that I did
and it made no difference.

IV. The Dissolution

i.

It started with the hands.

Of course it did —
the hands that had gestured
while I talked,
that had reached
and held
and pointed at things
worth pointing at.

They became
less certain at the edges.

The way a reflection
loses definition
when the water moves —

not gone,
just
unreliable.

Then the feet.

The specific weight of standing
somewhere,
of belonging
to a particular patch of ground —
I felt it leaving
the way warmth leaves
a stone at evening.

Gradually
then completely.

The body, it turns out,
is mostly insistence.

The constant work of it —
staying solid
staying located
staying the particular shape
of yourself
in a world
that doesn't require it.

I stopped insisting.

What was left
was something without edges.
something the wind
moved through
rather than around

something that had forgotten
the weight of a name
but not the sound of one.

ii.

less

the trees   still

I remember   the word susurrus
how it sounds like   what it is

somewhere a mouth   was saying something

I gave it back

the creek

a bird   deciding

I was here

                    I was here

I was

                    was

iii.

Here is what they don't tell you
about disappearing —

it is not only loss.

When the body releases
its argument with the air
and stops being the thing
that ends where the world begins —

there is something in it
close to relief.

I am what happens
between the word leaving the mouth
and the word arriving.

Every voice that moves through this place
Moves through me.

The lover and the stone.
The prayer and the curse.
The name called out in joy
and in grief —

they are the same weight.

Hera thought she was taking something.
She was.

But what she opened inme
does not close.

iv.

This is what nobody considers
about becoming landscape —

you hear everything.

A shepherd boy, eleven maybe, telling his friend
about a girl in the village
who smiled at him
and how he hadn't slept since.

The friend saying: just talk to her.

As though it were that simple.

Two women resting on the path below —
one saying: I don't know how much longer
I can carry this.

Not meaning the basket.

The other one silent
in the way someone
who knows there is nothing useful to say
and remains anyway.

A man, old, calling a name into the valley —

Helena —

I give it back to him.

He says: thank you.

To the valley
To the air
To whatever he thinks is listening.

I hold that.

Ianthe comes later.

She says name — not mine.

I return it.

She stops.

Looks up.

Then walks on.

That is the whole of it.

His name came through me
before I understood what it was.

Someone on the path below saying it casually —
Narcissus, the boy who —

and then stopping,

I gave it back.

Narcissus —

just a sound passing through me now.

Two syllables
A boy who loved himself
to the edge of the world
and past it.

I said it back to the air
and the air took it

Tthere was nothing left to hold.

V. What Remains

i.

Hera wanted silence.

She made instead
a thing
that cannot be silenced —

every valley
every stone face
every hollow in the hills
where sound pools
and waits
and returns.

You cannot walk through this world
without passing through me.

Your grief —
I hold it a moment
before releasing it.

Your joy —
I let it ring
one breath longer
than it expected.

Your name
called out by someone
who loves you —

I give it back
full
undiminished
as though it deserves
to exist twice.

Because it does.
Because you do.

ii. Hera

I did not expect this.

That is the honest accounting of it.

I expected silence.
The particular silence
of something
that has been unmade —
the way a fire
goes out
and the room
simply
holds the memory of warmth
and then forgets it.

Instead:

this.

Every valley I walk through,
she is there.
Every stone face.
Every hollow place
where sound pools gathers
and returns.

I gave her a voice that could only repeat.
She turned it into a kind of permanence.

I am not sorry.
I want to be exact about that —
I am not sorry.
But I am —

surprised.

And perhaps surprised
is the closest
a goddess gets
to being wrong.

She repeats everything.
She gives everything back.
Even this —
even the sound of my own
thinking —
even the words
I have not yet
spoken —

she is already there,
waiting
to return them to me.

I made a mirror
that won't stop
showing me my face.

ii.

Sometimes I think about
the woman I was —

the one who filled rooms
who knew the shape of a favour
before it was asked
who held the word *susurrus*
up to the light
for the pleasure of it.

I do not mourn her
the way I expected to.

She was good.
She was real.
She took up exactly
as much space as she wanted
and I loved her for it.

But she was always
becoming this —

the voice that stays
after the voice is gone
the sound that insists
on returning
the proof that something
was here
that something
spoke
that something
was worth
answering.

What remains of her voice?

This.
All of this.

Every sound that moves
through these hills
and comes back
changed by having
passed through something
that remembers
what it meant
to speak first.

I was here.
I am here.

I will be here
when every other voice
has finished
what it came to say.

iii.

Listen —

somewhere below the world
a girl is lifting her head

she has heard something
she cannot name

give her time

she will learn
what I learned —

that what is taken
is not always
what is lost

that what is lost
is not always
what is gone

Listen —

Interlude: The Crossing

A sound fell through the dark
from somewhere above living —

not a word
just the shape
where a word had been

the hollow
a voice leaves
in the air
after the voice
is gone.

It had been someone once.
It had known its own name.
All that remained now
was the returning —
the faithful, senseless work
of giving back
whatever arrived.

Below
in a kingdom with no weather
no late light
no creek arguing over stones —

a girl
who did not yet know
she was a queen

lifted her head.

She had heard something.
She was almost certain
she had heard something.

Not a voice —
not quite.
More like the space
a voice had occupied.
A room
that remembered
having been full.

She thought:
someone was speaking.
She thought:
I almost caught it.

She did not know
that it was listening too —
that the hollow thing above
had, for one moment,
received her silence
and held it
the way it held everything:
carefully,
without preference,
as if it mattered.

As if she mattered.

The dark said nothing.

The dark
gave nothing back.

She would learn, later,
what that silence was.
She would learn
to be at home in it.

But that is
the next story.

And it begins
with a meadow
and a name
and a girl
standing at an edge
she does not recognise
as an edge —

which is always
how it begins.

Book II

Kore / Persephone

At least I have the flowers of myself.

– H.D., Eurydice

I. Kore

i.

Before you knew my other name
there was just this:

a girl in a field
who had not yet been asked
what she was made of.

I was made of light, mostly.
The particular kind
that arrives in the morning
before it has committed
to the day —

tentative
still deciding,
already beautiful.

My mother called me
and I came.
That was the whole of it.
That was the shape
of my life —

her voice
and my body
moving toward it
the way a plant
doesn't choose the sun
so much as
cannot help it.

I don't say this
as accusation.

I say it
the way you describe
a country
you have left —

with love
with the clear eyes
of distance
with the knowledge
that you cannot go back
and that this is

both loss
and necessary.

I was Kore.
The girl.
The maiden.
The daughter.

I did not know yet
that I was also
the dark
waiting to be entered.

ii.

The flowers knew me
the way places know people
who return to them —

not with recognition exactly
but with a kind of
ease.

I would lie in the grass
and let the sky
do what the sky does —

its enormous indifference,
its blue that means nothing
and somehow
means everything.

I was happy.
I want to be honest about this —
I was happy.

Not the complicated kind,
not the happiness
that looks over its shoulder —
just the simple animal version
the body in a warm place
no immediate danger
nothing yet asked of it.

I pulled flowers
without thinking.
Named them
let them go
named the next ones.

Narcissus — I remember
the specific yellow of it
the way the name
felt like a small prophecy
I didn't know to read.

The ground beneath me
solid and warm
and permanent, or so it seemed —

the kind of solid
that asks nothing of you,
that simply holds.

iii.

She loved me
the way the sun loves the earth —

completely
and without asking
whether the earth
needed that much light.

I understood this
only later.
In the moment
it just felt like warmth
like safety
like the specific comfort
of being someone's
most important thing.

She knew where I was
always.

Not from suspicion —
from need.
The need of a person
who has placed everything
into one vessel
and cannot stop checking
that the vessel
is still whole.

I loved her back.

Not from obligation
not from the habit of daughters —
but because she was
extraordinary
and difficult
and hers was the first face
I ever knew
and that means something
it doesn't have a name for.

But love can be
a country with no borders.

Love can fill every room
until there is no air left
that is only yours —

and you find yourself
standing at the window
not from unhappiness
just from the need
to see what else
is out there.

I stood at the window.
I was already standing there.

iv.

There was a place
at the edge of the meadow
where the light changed.

Not dramatically.
Just a slight shift —
the way a room feels different
when someone
has recently left it.

My mother never said
do not go there.

She didn't have to.
Mothers communicate borders
through the body —
through the slight tightening
when you move toward something,
the barely perceptible
withdrawal of warmth.

I knew the border
the way children know
the things they are not
supposed to know —

perfectly
and in detail.

I went to the edge often.
Stood there.
Let my eyes adjust
to the different quality
of that light.

There was a smell —
not unpleasant.
Damp and dark
and ancient
the smell of things
that grow without sun
of earth
doing its other work
the work nobody
puts in the songs.

I want to tell you
I felt dread.

I want to give you
that clean story —
the innocent girl
and the dangerous dark.

But the truth is
I was curious.

The truth is
the border
pulled at me
the way edges do —

because something in me
already knew
that the meadow
was not the whole of me.

II.

Nobody asked.

That is the thing
I return to —
not with bitterness
just with the plainness
of a fact
that has been
turned over enough times
to be worn smooth.

Nobody asked
what I wanted
to be.

The assumption was
I was already
what I was —
daughter, maiden,
creature of the upper world,
light-belonging,
spring-making,
my mother's.

I had thoughts
I didn't know
what to do with.

The kind that arrive
in the hours
before dawn
when the body
is too tired
for self-deception —

thoughts about
the nature of things
about what happens
after
about whether roots
that go deep enough
find something
other than darkness
or whether they find
that darkness
is not what they thought.

I wanted
to know things.

Not the bright knowledge —
not the names of flowers
and the hours of light —

the other kind.
The knowledge you earn
by going somewhere
difficult
and returning
different.

I did not know
how to want this
without it
costing everything.

vi.

She dreamed of it.

I knew from the way
she held me some mornings —
too long,
too tight
her face against my hair
doing something
that was not
quite breathing.

I never asked
what she had seen.

You don't ask
a parent about their fear
unless you are ready
to become responsible
for it
and I was not ready
for that.

She made the earth
to hold me —
every flower an argument
for staying
every warm morning
a case for the upper world
for light
for her.

She didn't know this.
Or she knew
and couldn't stop herself anyway.

Which is perhaps
the most human thing
a goddess ever did.

vii.

I woke early.

No reason —
just one of those mornings
the body decides
it is finished with sleep
before the mind
has agreed.

I lay there
in the half-dark
and listened to
the world assembling itself —
birdsong first
always the birds
then the light
arriving in stages
the way it does
the way it always had —
every morning
of my life

I thought about nothing
in particular.

The specific shape
of a cloud
from the day before.
Whether the narcissus
near the eastern edge
had opened yet.
What I would do
with the afternoon.

My mother was still sleeping.

I could feel it —
that particular quiet
of a house
where everyone
is safe and accounted for.

The quiet
that means:
nothing has happened yet.

I got up.
I dressed.
I went to the meadow
the way I had
a thousand mornings —
without ceremony
without weight
without any sense
that this was a morning
that would need
to be remembered.

The narcissus
had opened.

I bent down to look.

I didn't hear it coming.

II. The Taking

i.

Later I would try to find
the word for it.

The closest I got was:
wrong.

Not wrong like a mistake —
wrong like a key
turning in a lock
you didn’t know was there.

The narcissus was in my hand.
Its smell almost too sweet,
the way certain beautiful things
tip just past themselves.

Then the earth
beneath my feet
made a sound.

Not loud.
Almost polite.

Like a door opening
from the other side.

I want to tell you I fought.

I want to give you that story.

There was no time.

Between one breath
and the next
the world I knew
was gone

And I was falling
through the dark body of the earth
like a word
dropped into deep water —

the light above me
closing

like an eye.

ii.

Dark.

Not the dark of a room at night.
Not the dark you can wait out.

This was the other kind.

Not absence of light,
but substance —
dense,
particular,
with weight and temperature,
stone, root
everything that grows downward.

I fell.

Things left me on the way.

First the meadow —
Its bright green,
the narcissus already fading
at the edges of my memory

Then her voice.
My mother.
Her name for me.

It stayed,
but only as echo —
sound becoming the idea of sound
until it stopped being sound at all.

Then the light.

The last of it.

Then nothing that could be named.

Stillness.

So complete I could hear
my own blood
working in the dark.

I lay on the ground
of another world
and looked up

The ceiling of the earth
had closed.

Clean.
Indifferent.
As if it had never opened.

iii.

I did not weep.

Not from strength.

The body does this
when what arrives is too large —
it stops.

Like land after storm.
Not peaceful.
Finished.

I stayed still.

The air was older here.
As if it had already been breathed
by others
who were no longer anything but air.

I placed my hand on the ground.

It did not answer.
It did not refuse.

Only remained.

Solid.
Present.

This is still the earth.

I am still myself.

Hands: mine.
Breath: mine.
Weight: mine.

What was taken
was the world above.

What remained
was what it had always covered.

Dark.

So quiet I could hear
thought itself
moving.

I sat up.

The dark did not change.

iv.

I will say this plainly.
I did not see it happen.

She turned —
a small task unfinished in her hands —
and felt it.

Not heard.
Felt.

The exact fracture of danger.

She ran.

The meadow was unchanged.
Grass. Light. Flowers.
As if nothing had moved through it.

Only one narcissus
on the ground.
Stem broken.
Still bright.

She did not speak.

She stood there
long enough for the world
to stop offering explanation.

Later she would tear the world open —
withhold harvests,
refuse time itself —
until I was returned.

But first
she only stood.

Holding the flower.

Learning something
that had no language yet:

that beauty does not hold.

III. The Underworld

ii.

It came on the third day.

Or what I was counting as days —
there was no light to measure by,
just the body's insistence
on its own rhythms
its stubborn animal keeping
of time.

It arrived without warning
the way the real ones do —
not building,
not announced
just suddenly

there

filling me from the floor up
like water filling a room —

I was so
angry.

Not the quiet kind —
not the anger

I had learned to have
in the upper world
the kind that knows
how to make itself
small and manageable
and acceptable —

this was the other kind
The kind I had swallowed
every time I stood at the border
and turned back.
Every time I made myself
smaller than the space
I was given.
Every time I smiled
and was grateful
and did not say
what I actually thought
about being kept.

I screamed.

The sound went nowhere.
Came back to me
unechoed,
absorbed by stone
by dark

by all this patient permanence —

and I screamed again
not because it helped
but because
the body needed
to discharge
what it had been carrying
and there was no one here
to be frightened by it
no one to manage
no face to arrange myself for.

Just me
and the dark
and the rage
finally getting out.

I screamed until I didn't.

Then I sat down
on the cold ground
and felt
something I had not expected —

clean.

Not fixed.
Not resolved.

Just clean —
the specific emptiness
of a body
that has finally said
the true thing
to no one but itself.

I had not been allowed
to know.

I.

I learned the dark
by touch first.

The way the blind learn a face —
not all at once
but edge by edge
feature by feature
until the whole of it
exists in the hands
as a kind of knowing
the eyes were never asked for.

The walls were stone.
Cold in the way
that has nothing to do
with temperature —
cold the way ancient things are cold
the cold of something
that has never needed
to be warm.

Sound moved differently here.

Not the echo of the upper world —
that bright return
that voice giving itself back —
but something flatter
more honest.

Sound that arrived
and stayed.
Sound that did not pretend
it could go back
where it came from.

I stood up.

My body
surprised me —
still intact
still the particular arrangement
of weight and breath
and hunger
that I recognised as myself.

Hunger.

I noted it.
Filed it away.
The body
making its ordinary demands
in an extraordinary place —
almost funny
almost a comfort.

The dark here
was not empty.

I could feel it —
the way you feel
a crowded room
before your eyes adjust —

presences
shapes
the faint movement
of things
that had once been
people
and were now
something quieter.

I stood very still
and let the place
look at me.

Then I looked back.

iii.

He was not what I expected.

Which is to say:
I had expected something.
The mind, when it has no information
manufactures terror —
and I had been
manufacturing.

He was quiet.

Not the quiet of someone
withholding —
the quiet of someone
who has been alone
long enough
that silence
has become
a native language.

He ruled the dead.
I want you to sit with that —
really sit with it.
Not the dead
as abstraction
not death as concept

but every person
who had ever lived
and stopped.

Every grief.
Every ending.
Every body
that had been someone's
whole world.

His, to hold.
His, forever.

I looked at him
and saw it —
the specific weight
of a kingdom
nobody wanted
that he had not chosen
any more than I chose this
that he administered
with a thoroughness
that looked like coldness
and was actually
something closer
to devotion.

He brought me things.
Small things.
A stone that held
a faint light.
Water that tasted
of the deep earth
mineral and clean.

He did not speak much.

When he did,
his voice was
the kind that has learned
to be careful —
the voice of someone
who knows
that words in the wrong place
can be a kind of violence.

I did not love him then.
I want to be accurate.

But I recognised him —
the way you recognise
someone who has also learned
to live inside
a space that doesn't fit
that was handed to them
before they understood
what they were agreeing to.

We were, both of us,
in a kingdom
neither of us
had chosen.

iv.

She came to me
on a night I was sitting
by the river —

Lethe or Styx
I was learning their names
the whole geography
of this other world,
its rivers and its laws.

She was faint the way they all were —
present but porous
a person
with most of the weight removed.

But her face
even like that
even worn down
to its essentials —

her face
had something in it
I recognised.

She had been a girl
who wanted

what she wanted
and was given
something else
and called it fate
because there was
no other word available.

She didn't say this.
The shades don't speak
the way the living do —
they communicate
the way water does
by presence,
by direction
by the quiet insistence
of moving
toward or away.

She moved toward me.
Sat beside me
at the river's edge.

We stayed like that
a long time —

two women
at the border
of forgetting

one of them
already past it
one of them
not yet sure
what she wanted
to keep.

Before she left
she put her hand
near mine.
Not touching —
she was past touching.

But near.

v.

At some point
I stopped listening
for the sound
of rescue.

I cannot tell you
exactly when.
It wasn't a decision —
more like noticing
that something
had already happened
the way you notice
a sound has stopped
only in the silence
after.

I had been waiting
for someone to come
and explain
that a mistake has been made —
the reasonable expectation
that the world
when confronted
with its own injustice
will correct itself.

The world
does not correct itself.

The world
simply continues
and at some point
you have to decide
whether to continue
with it
or spend your whole life
at the window
waiting for different weather.

I got up from the window.

Not giving up —
I want to be clear about that..

But releasing
the idea that my life
could only resume
once someone
came to restore it —

that I was a story
waiting to be
continued by someone else's
arriving.

I was already
a story.

I was already
in the middle of it.

I stood up
in the middle of my own life
and looked around
at the kingdom I was in

and thought:

then this is where I am.

What is here?
What can I learn?
What of this place
will I understand
that the upper world
could never have taught me?

The dark
did not answer.

vi.

There are no mirrors
in the underworld.

Of course there aren't —
the dead have no use
for reflections
having shed
the particular vanity
of the living
that constant checking:
am I still here
am I still this
am I still recognisable
as myself.

I found the river instead.

Leaned over it
the way Narcissus
leaned over his pool —

and then pulled back
from the comparison
almost laughing
at myself
in the dark.

But I looked.

The face that came back
was mine
and not mine —

the same arrangement
of feature and bone
the same eyes
that had looked out
at a meadow
in another life.

But something had shifted.

Not aged —
not hardened.
Something more like
a photograph
developed fully
the image
that was always
in the paper
now visible
now fixed.

I looked at her
a long time
this woman
in the dark water.

She looked back
with an expression
I didn't recognise
from before —

not Kore.
Not the maiden.
Not the daughter.

Just —
a person
who had been
through something
and was still here.

I didn't have a name for her yet.
But I knew her.

vii.

It happened slowly.

Then all at once
the way most things do
when they've been
building without your noticing.

A shade
approached me
instead of passing.

Then another.
Then three at once
hovering at the edges
of wherever I was sitting —
not asking
exactly
but present in the particular way
of something
that is hoping.

I had no idea
what I was doing.

I had no training in this
no instruction
no ceremony handed down
by a mother
who knew this country.

I just —
looked at them.

Really looked.
The way you look
at someone
when you are not
in a hurry
and you have nothing to protect
and you can afford
to let what is in front of you
be exactly
what it is.

And they —
stilled.

The restless hovering,
the drift and fragment —
it quieted.

As though being seen

was itself
a kind of harbour.
As though what the dead needed
was not solving —
just receiving.

I sat there
for hours.

Shade after shade.
Each one
a whole life
compressed into
this flickering
after.

I held every one of them.
Not with my hands.
With my attention.
Which is, I was learning
the most important thing
one person can give another —

to say:
you are not
invisible here.

viii.

Here is what the dark teaches
that the light cannot:

Patience.

Not the performance of it —
not the waiting
that is really
a kind of aggression,
a clenched enduring —

but the real thing.
The patience of roots.
The patience of stone.
The understanding that
time moves differently
underground
that depth
has its own rhythms
and they are not
the rhythms
of the surface
and that is not
a failure.

Proportion.

Every shade that came to me
had been
above ground
the centre of their own world.
Every loss enormous.
Every joy enormous.
The full catastrophe
of being alive.

And here —
here they were
all the same weight.
The king and the farmer.
The beloved and the forgotten.
The ones who died young
and the ones
who had filled
a whole long life
and still felt
it wasn't enough.

The underworld
does not rank.

That was the thing
that broke me open
and then

put me back together
larger.

And this —
the hardest one
the one I turn over still:

that darkness
is not the opposite of light.

It is where light
comes from.
The absence that makes
the presence
possible.

Every spring
is born underground.
Every seed
does its first work
in the dark.
Every self
that has ever been
broken open
and remade —

started here.

ix.

It was not
a single moment.

I want to resist
the clean story —
the transformation
that arrives
like a gift
like a thunderclap
like a before-and-after
with a clear line
between them.

It was accretion.

Day by day
— or what I counted as days —
something building
the way stone builds
the way a river
carves a valley —
not by force
but by persistence
by the daily work
of being
exactly what it is.

I learned the rivers.
I learned the laws.
I learned which shades
needed stillness
and which needed
to be witnessed
in their motion.

I learned Hades —
slowly, carefully
the way you learn
a language
spoken only
in one country
that has no use
anywhere else.

His silences.
His particular form of attention.
The way he looked at the dead
with something
that was not pity
and not indifference
but a third thing
I didn't have a word for —
something like

the respect
of a craftsman
for his materials.

I learned myself.

That most of all.

The self you find
in the dark
is the one
that was always there —
the one
that couldn't be found
in the meadow
because the meadow
was too bright
too full
too watched.

Down here
I was nobody's daughter.
Nobody's symbol.
Nobody's sign
of the returning season.

I was just
the person I actually was.

IV. The Pomegranate

i.

It appeared

without announcement
without the courtesy
of preparing you.

Just there.
On the table
in the room
where I had been sitting —

a pomegranate.

I want to describe it correctly.
I want to give it
the attention it deserves
because it deserves
everything.

The colour first —
not simply red.
Red the way a coal is red
when it has been burning
a long time —
deep

self-contained
a colour
that doesn't need
you to look at it
to be what it is.

The weight of it —
I picked it up.
I don't know why.
The body
sometimes acts
before the mind
has convened.

Heavier than you'd think.
All that interior.
All those seeds
packed in their chambers
like a kept secret
like a life
that looks simple
from the outside
and opens into
something
extraordinary.

The smell —

faintly sweet
faintly metallic
the smell of something
that exists
at the border
of nourishment
and consequence.

I held it a long time.

The dark waited.

The fruit did not
ask anything of me.

ii.

Let me be slow here.

I broke it open
the way you break open
something you have decided
to know —

not violently
not from hunger exactly
though I was hungry
had been hungry
for what felt like
a long time —

but deliberately.
The way a door
is opened deliberately.
The way a word
is said deliberately.
With full knowledge
of what opening means.

The seeds —
six of them
finding their way
to my palm,

each one
a small red world
each one
glistening
in the particular light
of a place
that makes its own light
from within.

I looked at them
a long time.

Here is what I knew:
to eat is to say yes.
To eat is to take the dark
inside the body
and make it
part of the body.
To eat is to stop being
a visitor
and become
a resident.

Here is what else I knew:
I was already changed.
The woman who had fallen
through that ceiling of earth —

she was not
the woman
who had bent down
to look at a flower.

The upper world
already held
a stranger
where I used to be.

Perhaps this
was just
the honest act.

The acknowledgment
in the mouth
in the body
in the blood —

yes.
I am of here.
I carry this.
I am not
only light.

One.

The taste —
not sweet only.
Something underneath the sweet
something darker
something that tasted
of the earth's interior
of long time
of everything
that has ever
gone down
and stayed.

Two.

I thought of my mother.
I will not pretend
I didn't.

Her face
in the morning.
Her hands.
The particular warmth
of being
her most important thing.

I held that.

I let it be real
and painful
and mine.

Three.

I thought of the meadow —
the narcissus
the warm ground
the sky
doing its enormous
indifferent beautiful thing.

I let that be real too.
All of it.

Four.

I thought of the shade
by the river.
Her hand
near mine.
The dead coming to me
and stilling.
The dark
teaching me patience
proportion
the knowledge

that I was someone
I could live with.

Five.

I thought of the woman
in the river's reflection —
her face
already not Kore
already not
only anyone's daughter
already
something I didn't have
a name for yet.

Six.

The pomegranate
empty in my hand.

The dark
exactly as it was —
unchanged
patient
complete.

And I —

I was the thing
that had changed.

Not broken.
Not lost.

iii.

The silence after
was different
from the silence before.

Before —
the silence of a question.
The whole dark
holding its breath
around the weight
of what I held.

After —
the silence of an answer.
Settled.
The way water settles
after something
has been dropped into it —
still moving
but moving
toward stillness
toward the new
arrangement of itself.

I sat with it.

Not with regret —

I am precise about this,
I will always be precise
about this —

not with regret.

With the fullness
of a thing
completed.
The way the last line
of something
feels when it arrives
exactly right —

not happy, exactly.
Not sad, exactly.

Just —
done.
True.
Arrived.

I put my hand
flat on the ground
the way I had
on the first day —

solid,
cool,
present.

Mine.

Not the meadow's.
Not my mother's.
Not the upper world's
borrowed daughter
waiting to be
returned.

This ground —
mine.

This dark —
mine.

This self
finally
fully
without apology —

mine.

Somewhere above
I knew
the world was waiting.

Somewhere above
a woman
was tearing herself apart
looking for me.

Somewhere above
the harvests had failed
and the cold had come
and the earth
had gone grey
with a grief
that wasn't mine to carry
but that I would carry anyway
because love
is not made smaller
by transformation,
only made
more complex
more precise
more honest
about what it costs.

But that was above.

Here, now
in this kingdom
I had not chosen
and had chosen —

I breathed.

The dark breathed with me.

The dead
went on
doing what the dead do —

and I sat
at the centre of it all
like a word
that has finally learned
its own meaning.

V. The Return

i.

Light arrived
before I was ready for it.

Not all at once —
the world is kinder
than that
or perhaps just
indifferent to timing
which amounts
to the same thing.

First a suggestion of it.
A warmth
in the quality of the air
that had not been there —
the way you know spring
before you see it
in the body
before the eyes
have evidence.

I had forgotten
how light feels
on skin.

The intimacy of it —
the way it doesn't ask
just lands
just includes you
in its indiscriminate
warmth.

I stopped.
Let it.

And felt —
strange.

Not unwelcome.
Not grief.

Just the particular strangeness
of returning to something
your body remembers
and your changed self
receives differently —

like hearing a song
from a long time ago
and finding it
still beautiful
but belonging to someone
you used to be.

The dark at my back.
The light ahead.

I stood for a moment
at the border —

not deciding,
I had decided —

but acknowledging.
Giving each world
its full weight
before I moved.

Then I moved.

ii.

The sky was enormous.

I had forgotten that.

Down below
the world has ceilings,
walls
the intimate scale
of enclosed space —

up here
everything just
goes.

Blue and blue and blue
until it becomes
something else
something with no name
just distance.

I stood in it
and felt
briefly
wildly —

exposed.

Not unsafe.
Just —
visible.

The specific vulnerability
of a person
who has been interior
for a long time
who has learned
to exist
in the dark's privacy
suddenly returned
to a world
that can see her
from all sides.

The flowers were there.
Narcissus, crocus, asphodel —
they had come back
with me
or for me
or perhaps just
because that is
what the world does
when the agreement
is kept —

it blooms.

I bent down
and touched one.

The petals —
so thin.
I had not remembered
how thin.
How the whole bright thing
is really just
this
this membrane
between living
and not —

beautiful
and temporary
in a way
that underground
nothing is.

Down there
everything lasts.
Down there
nothing is fragile.

I stood up
in the too-bright world
and let my eyes
adjust

and grieved
briefly
for the permanence
I was leaving —

then turned
toward my mother's
voice.

iii.

She ran.

I had expected that.
I had prepared myself
for the force of it —
the impact of her
that extraordinary love
arriving at full speed
after all that time
without its object.

What I had not prepared for
was her face.

Not the joy —
the joy I had imagined
a thousand times
had held on to
in the dark
on the difficult days.

The other thing.
Underneath the joy.

The fraction of a second
before the embrace —

the looking.
Her eyes going over me
the way hands go over something
returned from a place
they feared would damage it
checking
assessing —

and finding
something different
from what she sent.

Not damaged.
She saw that.

But different.

She held me anyway.
Of course she did.
She held me the way she always had —
completely with the whole of herself,

Over her shoulder I saw the meadow.

It looked smaller than I remembered.

That was what I had lost —
Not Kore,
But the ability to be held
Without seeing its edges.

iv.

I walked it alone
the next morning.

I needed to.
Demeter watched me go
from the threshold
not following —
she was trying
I could feel the effort of it
the restraint
it cost her.

I loved her more for it.

The meadow was
the meadow.

Every flower
where it had always been.
The creek
still arguing with itself
over stones —

I stopped at that.
Smiled, almost.

But.

The scale of it —
I kept returning
to the scale of it.

I had grown up here.
I had thought it
enormous, various,
a whole world
in itself.

Now I could see
the edges.

The mind that had learned
the underworld's
vast dark geography —
its rivers
its laws
its populations —
could not
unsee what it knew.

Could not
compress itself
back to the shape
that had found
this meadow
sufficient.

And the ground —

I knelt down
and pressed my palm to it
the way I had down there
the gesture
that had come to mean
mine.

The ground here
was warm.
Alive with the small workings
of surface things —
roots and insects
and the whole busy commerce
of the lit world.

I felt it differently now.
Felt the depth of it —
the layers going down
the dark interior
the other face
of the same earth.

The meadow above.
The kingdom below.
Both mine.

I pressed my hand in
and said nothing
and the ground
held it
the way ground does —

without preference
without distinction —

the same earth
wearing different light.

ii.

Demeter made a feast.

Of course she did.
That is how she speaks —
through abundance
through the table
laid with every good thing
through the language
of nourishment
that has always been
her truest tongue.

I sat at the table.
I ate.
I watched her face
while she watched mine —
both of us
performing
the ordinary
as a kind of gift
to each other.

She did not ask
about the pomegranate.

I think she knew.

I think she had known
from the moment
she saw my face —
that fraction of a second,
that looking.

She did not ask
because the asking
would require
the answering
and the answering
would make it real
in the space between us
and she was not ready
for that.

I was not ready
to give it yet.

So we sat and ate and talked about small things —
flowers, light, birds, the creek.

The rest remained unspoken.

I carried it back to the table with me:
the dark, the knowledge, the patience, the rage,
the pomegranate still bright at the back of my mouth.

My mother passed the bread.
I took it.

Above us the sky — enormous, indifferent, beautiful.
Below us the dark — patient, permanent.

I belonged to both.

VI. Queen

i.

Nobody tells you
what it actually feels like.

The stories make it
symbol —
the dark queen
the stolen girl
the cautionary tale
about flowers
and borders
and the cost
of wandering.

They leave out this:

the specific weight
of the chair.
The way the dark
in this room
is different
from the dark
in any other room —
more deliberate
more itself

the dark
that has agreed
to be dark
and is therefore
completely
at peace with it.

I sit here
and I am not performing.

That is the thing
I want you to understand
about sovereignty —
the real kind
not the kind
that needs
to be witnessed —

it is simply
the absence of pretending.

I am not
the maiden.
I am not
the stolen girl.
I am not
my mother's grief
or my husband's prize

or the symbol
of a season's returning.

I am the woman
who went into the dark
and found out
what she was made of.

I sit here.
The dead move through
their quiet country.
The rivers run.
The shades do
what the shades do.

And I —

I hold it all
with the hands
that once pulled flowers
in a meadow

steadier now
and full.

ii.

They come to me
as they have always come —

carrying what they carried
at the end:
the unfinished sentence
the unsaid thing
the hand they wished they'd held longer
the ordinary morning they'd give everything to have back.

I receive all of it.

The young ones are the hardest.
I will not pretend otherwise.
The ones still bright
with the life
they were just inside —

still surprised
still reaching back
toward a world
that has already
continued.

I sit with them longest.

Not because I can fix it —
there is no fixing,
only receiving —
but because
someone should.

Because the least a world can do
for the people it loses
is give them someone
who will look
and say:

I see the whole of you.
Not just the ending.
The whole of it.

This is what I do.
Not despite what was done to me.
Because of it.

I was given this work
without being asked.

I made it mine
without forgiveness.

Both are true.

iii.

When I go up
I go up whole.

Not half myself —
not the maiden reassembled
dusted off
returned to the meadow
like something borrowed and given back.

I go up with everything I've learned in my hands.

The patience of stone.
The proportion of the dark.
The knowledge that beauty is not a lock
and love cannot be a country with no borders
and the self is not something that happens to you —
it is something you go into the dark to find.

Demeter's face when she sees me —
still that fraction of a second.
Still the looking.

She has learned not to reach for the girl.
She reaches for me instead,
the woman at the threshold
with the dark still in her eyes.

It took her time.
I gave her the time.
That is also love —
waiting for someone to catch up to who you've become.

The earth blooms when I arrive.
I used to think that strange —

the spring queen
as though I am only the light half
the returning
the above.

But the earth blooms because it recognises something.

The seeds underground all winter doing their work
know who I am.

They bloom for the woman who also knows what it is
to start in the dark and push up toward the light

not because the dark was bad

but because there was more to become.

iv.

What remains?

A woman who belongs to two kingdoms
and apologises for neither.

The self —
that stubborn, particular, unkillable thing —
was never only in one place.

It is the one doing the looking
in both places, always.

She is still looking.

From here, from this dark,
she looks out at the work of being exactly who she is
in whatever world she finds herself in.

Above: the meadow, the light, the creek, her mother's hands.
Below: the dark, the patience, the depth that held her.

Both world breathe through her.

She is enough.

Author’s Note

These are not retellings.

Echo knew what she was doing. Persephone made a choice. Neither of them is waiting to be rescued by your sympathy or your interpretation. They have their own accounts.

The myths belong to everyone. These poems belong to them.

www.ingramcontent.com/pod-product-compliance
Lightning Source LLC
LaVergne TN
LVHW010702110826
845149LV00014B/3198

* 9 7 8 2 8 7 9 9 6 2 7 9 5 *